This Orchard
book belongs to

_____

_____

_____

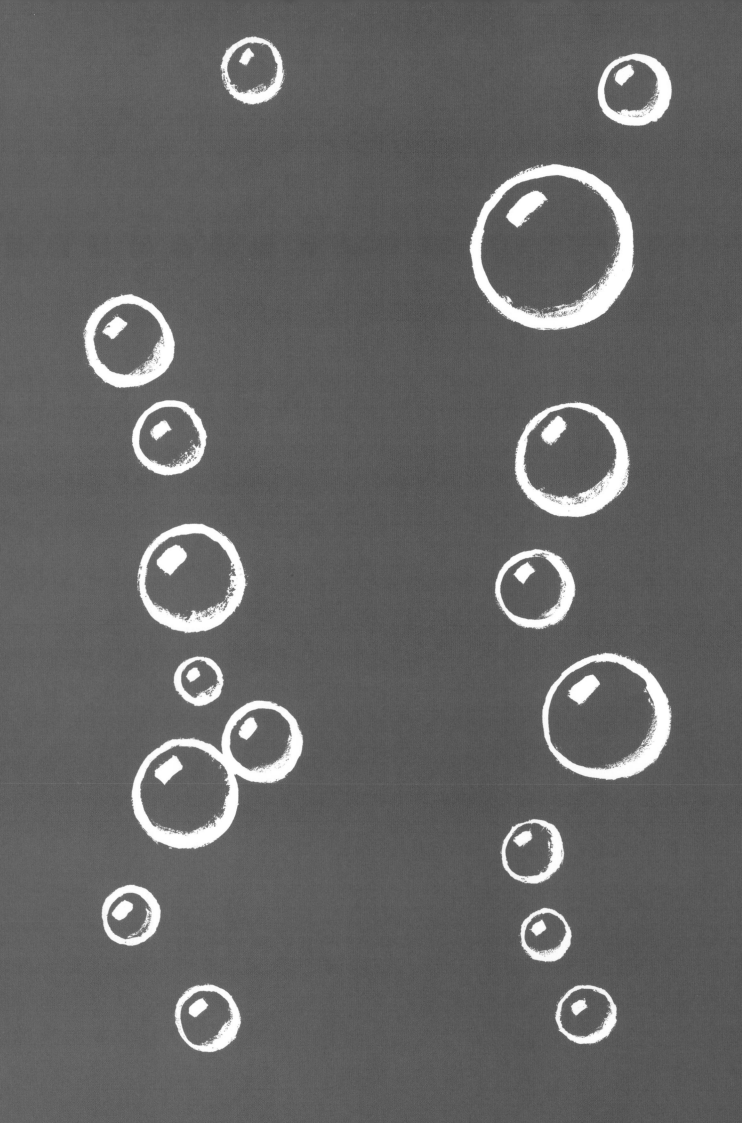

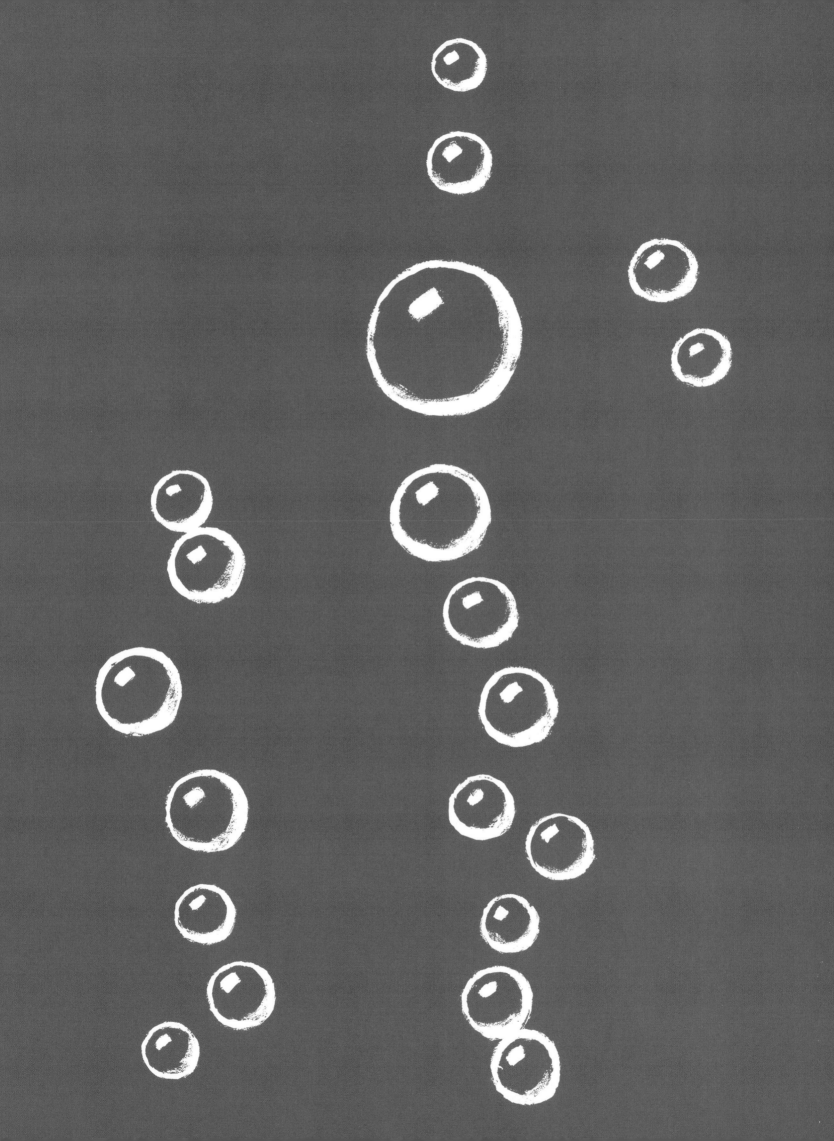

To Nicholas & Jonah
G. A.

Extra big thanks to Mandy & Jemima
love from David

ORCHARD BOOKS
Carmelite House
50 Victoria Embankment
London EC4Y 0DZ

First published in 1998 by Orchard Books
First published in paperback in 1999
Text © Purple Enterprises Ltd, a Coolabi company 1998 **coolabi**
Illustrations © David Wojtowycz 1998
A CIP catalogue record for this book is available from the British Library.

ISBN 978 1 84121 101 5

21

Printed in China

Orchard Books
An imprint of Hachette Children's Group
Part of The Watts Publishing Group Limited
An Hachette UK Company
www.hachette.co.uk

Commotion in the Ocean

Giles Andreae

Illustrated by David Wojtowycz

ORCHARD

Commotion in the Ocean

There's a curious commotion
At the bottom of the ocean
I think we ought to go and take a look.

You'll find every sort of creature
That lives beneath the sea
Swimming through the pages of this book.

There are dolphins, whales and penguins,
There are jellyfish and sharks,
There's the turtle and the big white polar bear.

But can you see behind the wrecks
And in-between the rocks?
Let's see if we can find who's hiding there …

Crab

The crab likes walking sideways
And I think the reason why,
Is to make himself look sneaky
And pretend that he's a spy.

Turtles

We crawl up the beach from the water
To bury our eggs on dry land,
We lay a whole batch
And then when they hatch
They scamper about in the sand.

pitter patter

pitter patter

squeak
squeak

click-click

Dolphins

The wonderful thing about dolphins
Is hearing them trying to speak,
But it's not "how d'you do?"
Like I'd say to you,
It's more of a "click-whistle-squeak!"

whistle

click

Angel Fish

Hello, I'm the angel fish, darling,
The prettiest thing in the sea,
What a shame there are no other creatures
As gorgeous and lovely as me!

jiggle

Jellyfish

The jellyfish just loves to jiggle
Which other fish think is quite dumb,
She knows that it's not all that useful
But jiggling's very good fun.

Shark

I swim with a grin up to greet you
See how my jaws open wide,
Why don't you come a bit closer?
Please, take a good look inside . . .

Swordfish

I love to chase after small fishes
It stops me from getting too bored,
And then when I start feeling hungry
I skewer a few on my sword.

tickle
tickle

Octopus

Having eight arms can be useful,
You may think it looks a bit funny,
But it helps me to hold all my children
And tickle each one on the tummy.

tee hee!

bzzz

bzzz

Stingray

At the bottom of the ocean
The stingray flaps his wings,
But don't you get too close to him
His tail really stings!

Lobster

Never shake hands with a lobster

It isn't a wise thing to do,

With a clippety-clap

And a snippety-snap

He would snip all your fingers in two.

Snippety snap

Clippety clap

Deep Sea

Miles below the surface
Where the water's dark and deep,
Live the most amazing creatures
That you could ever meet.

There are fish of all descriptions,
Of every shape and size,
Some have giant pointy teeth
And great big bulbous eyes.

Some of them can walk around
And balance on their fins,
But the strangest fish of all
Have glowing whiskers on their chins!

Blue Whale

There's no other beast on the planet
As big as the giant blue whale,
He measures a massive one hundred feet long
From his head to the tip of his tail.

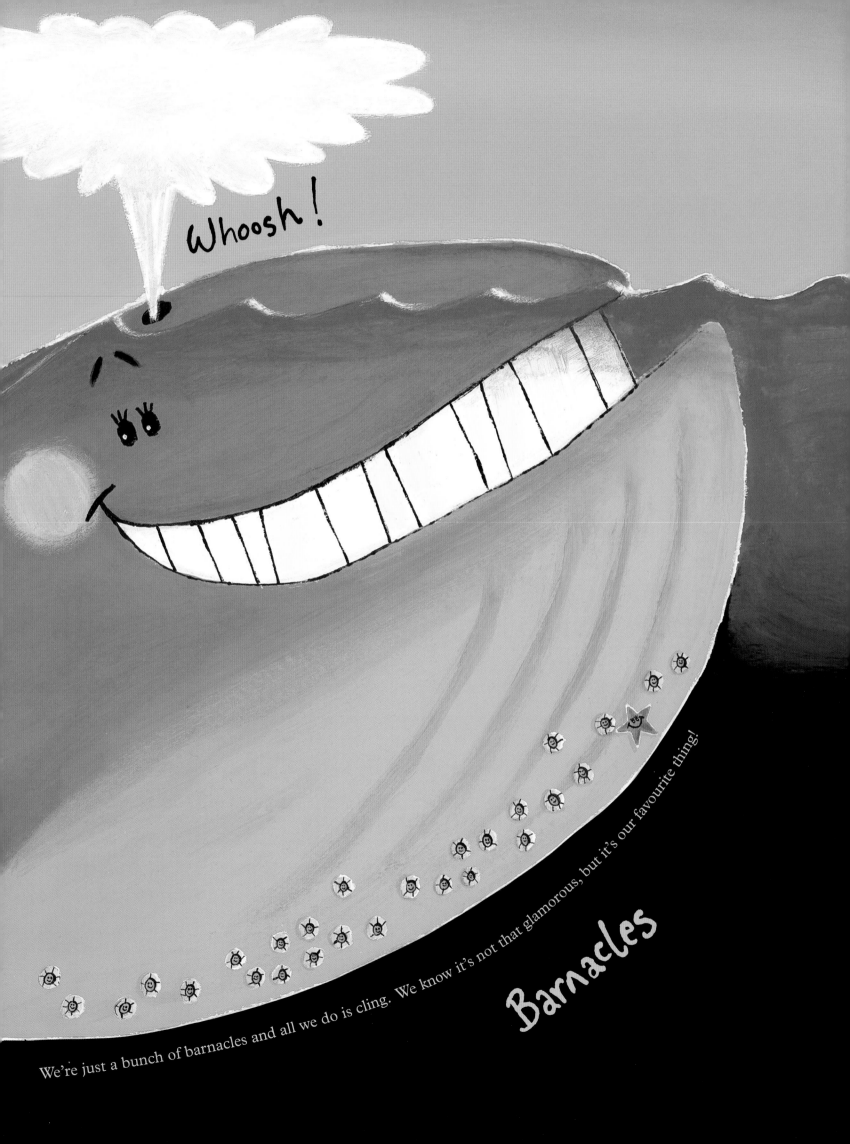

Walruses

Our bodies are covered with blubber
And our tusks are incredibly long,
We're grumpy and proud
And we bellow out loud
To show that we're mighty and strong.

Uuurggh

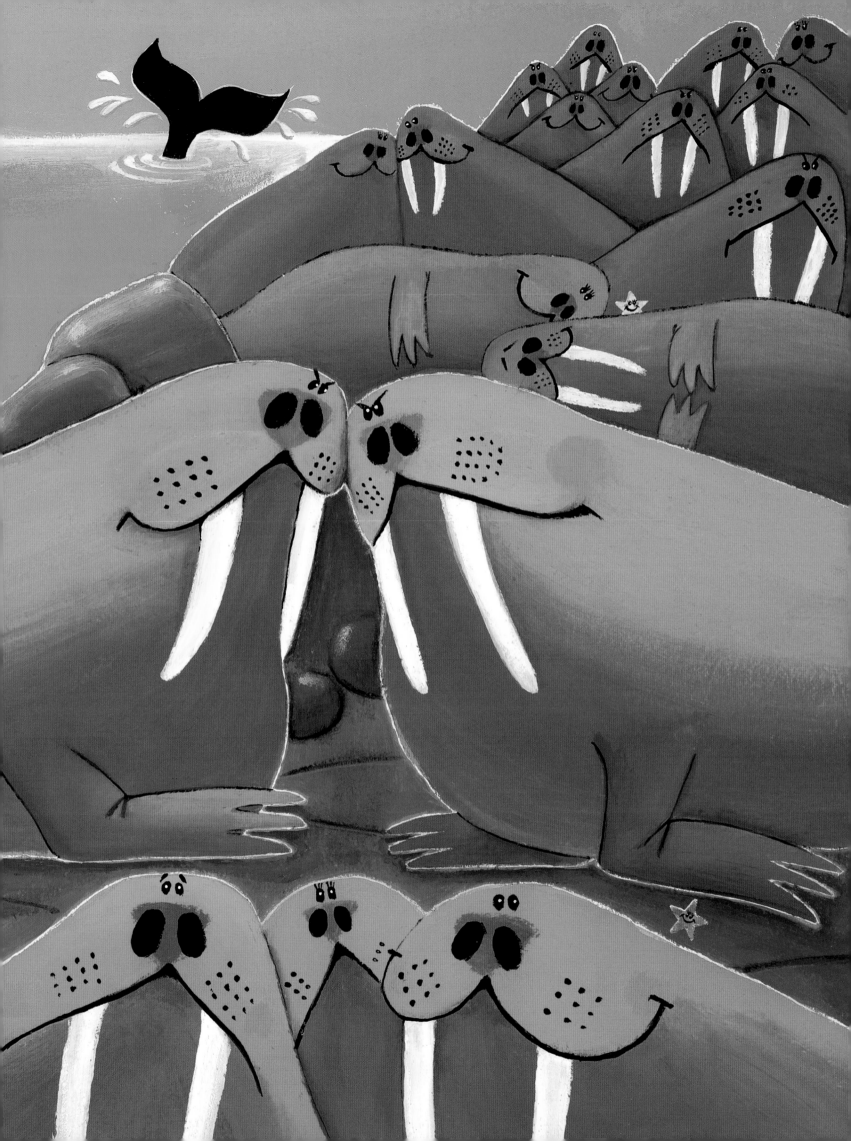

Wheeee!

splis

splash

splosh

Penguins

We waddle about on our icebergs,

Which makes our feet slither and slide,

And when we get close to the water

We leap with a splosh off the side.

Polar Bears

Deep out in the Arctic

The mummy polar bear

Snuggles up with all her children

As it's very cold out there.

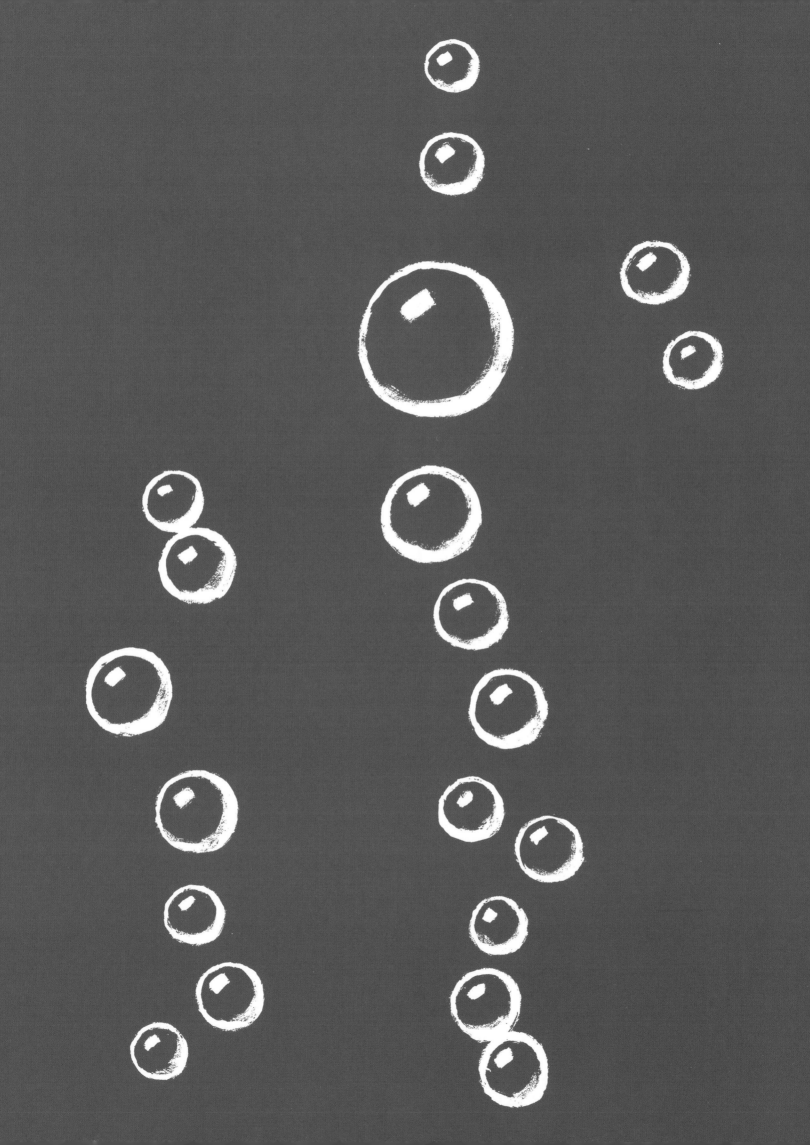